S0-CFQ-245

OLIVIA™
and the Snow Day

adapted by Farrah McDoogle
based on the screenplay written by Eryk Casemiro & Kate Boutilier
illustrated by Shane L. Johnson

Ready-to-Read

Simon Spotlight
New York   London   Toronto   Sydney

Based on the TV series OLIVIA™ as seen on Nickelodeon™

SIMON SPOTLIGHT

An imprint of Simon & Schuster Children's Publishing Division

1230 Avenue of the Americas, New York, New York 10020

Copyright © 2010 Silver Lining Productions Limited (a Chorion company). All rights reserved.

OLIVIA™ and © 2010 Ian Falconer. All rights reserved.

All rights reserved, including the right of reproduction in whole or in part in any form.

SIMON SPOTLIGHT, READY-TO-READ, and colophon are registered trademarks of Simon & Schuster, Inc.

For information about special discounts for bulk purchases, please contact Simon & Schuster

Special Sales at 1-866-506-1949 or business@simonandschuster.com.

Manufactured in the United States of America 1010 LAK

First Simon Spotlight edition, November 2010

2 4 6 8 10 9 7 5 3 1

Library of Congress Cataloging-in-Publication Data

McDoogle, Farrah.

Olivia and the snow day / adapted by Farrah McDoogle ; based on the screenplay written by

Eryk Casemiro & Kate Boutilier. — 1st ed.

p. cm. — (Ready-to-read)

"Based on the TV series, Olivia as seen on Nickelodeon"—Copyright page.

I. Casemiro, Eryk. II. Boutilier, Kate. III. Olivia (Television program) IV. Title.

PZ7.M478445701i 2010

[E]—dc22

2009047167

ISBN 978-1-4424-0813-5 (pbk)

ISBN 978-1-4423-3638-4 (hc)

"Look at all that 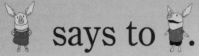," SNOW

 says to 🐷.

OLIVIA   IAN

"Will 🏫 be closed?" asks 🐷.

SCHOOL   IAN

"Listen to the 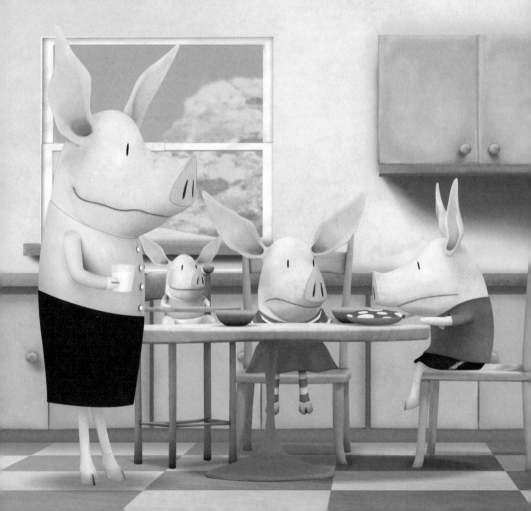 to find out," says 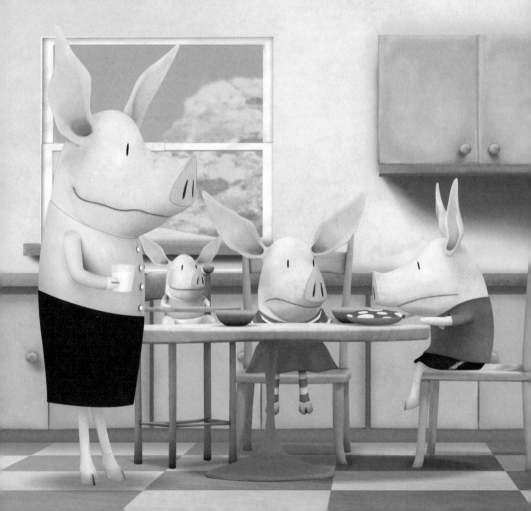.
RADIO MOTHER

 and turn up the .
OLIVIA IAN RADIO
The list of closed is
SCHOOLS
being read.

"Hampshire  is closed
today," says the  on the .
SCHOOL
MAN   RADIO
"Yippee!" shout  and .
OLIVIA   IAN
Today is a  day!
SNOW

"I will build a ," says .
SNOW FORT   IAN

He gets his , , and
HAT   BOOTS

.
MITTENS

"I have an even better idea," says . She gets her

OLIVIA

VIDEO CAMERA

"My viewers need facts about the ❄ day!"

SNOW

"I am live at the scene!"

says Reporter 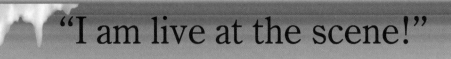.
OLIVIA

"Look at all this ❄!
SNOW

A 🏔 is taller than me!"
SNOWBANK

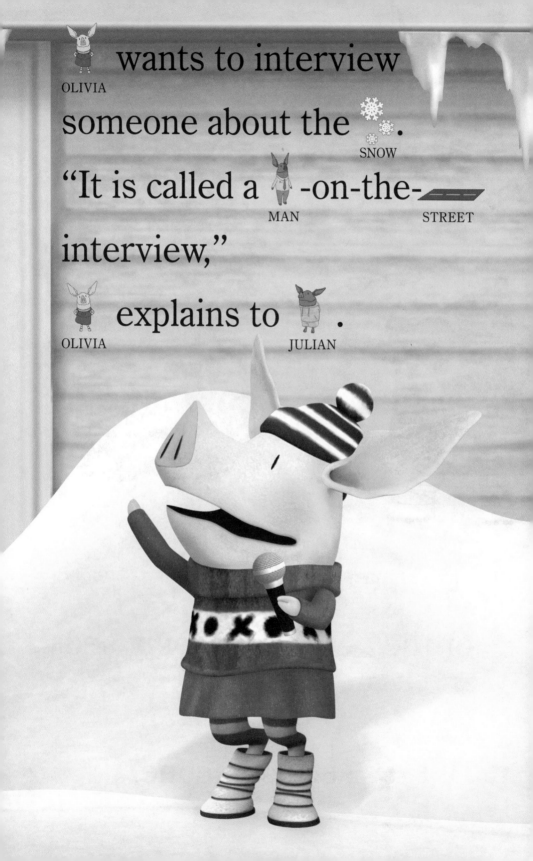

OLIVIA wants to interview someone about the SNOW.

"It is called a MAN-on-the-STREET interview," OLIVIA explains to JULIAN.

 does not see a

JULIAN   MAN

or the ▬. Julian only sees

STREET

.

SNOW

But sees someone.

OLIVIA

"Hello,  in the ,"
MAN   DRIVEWAY

calls  to her  .
OLIVIA   FATHER

"Do you have any thoughts

about the ?"
SNOW

"The is heavy," says

SNOW

.

FATHER

"How exciting!" says .

OLIVIA

thinks of an exciting story. "Hmm . . . have you seen the Abominable ?" 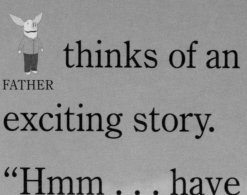 asks.

FATHER

SNOWMAN   FATHER

"Who is the Abominable ?" asks 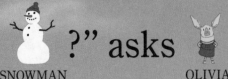 .

SNOWMAN   OLIVIA

"The Abominable is a

SNOWMAN

huge, hairy creature.

It makes huge in the

FOOTPRINTS

 ."

SNOW

 looks a little worried.

JULIAN

"Do not worry," says .

FATHER

Nobody has seen the

Abominable ."

SNOWMAN

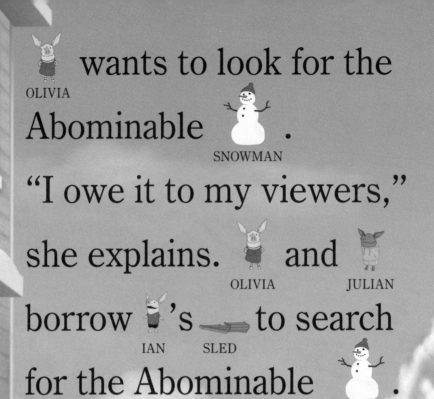 wants to look for the

Abominable .

OLIVIA

SNOWMAN

"I owe it to my viewers,"

she explains. OLIVIA and JULIAN

borrow IAN's SLED to search

for the Abominable SNOWMAN.

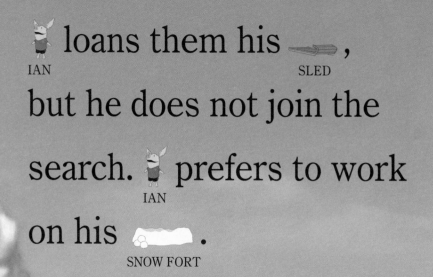

 loans them his ,
IAN   SLED

but he does not join the

search. prefers to work
        IAN

on his .
        SNOW FORT

"Something moved in the 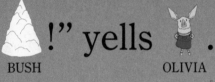!" yells .

BUSH   OLIVIA

But it is just .

PERRY

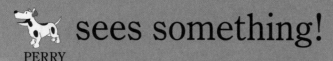 sees something!

PERRY

"Follow !" Olivia says.

PERRY

They see huge  !

FOOTPRINTS

"Roll the  ," whispers .

OLIVIA

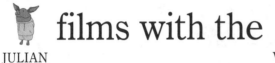 films with the  .

JULIAN   VIDEO CAMERA

"Did you hear that?"

OLIVIA

asks.

"The Abominable said

SNOWMAN

my name!"

The huge lead

FOOTPRINTS

to a tall .

SNOWBANK

Could it be the Abominable

 at last?

SNOWMAN

No! It is our friend !

HAROLD

He fell into the .

SNOWBANK

His made the .

SNOWSHOES   FOOTPRINTS

is sorry he is not
HAROLD

as exciting as the

Abominable . But
SNOWMAN

Reporter is not sorry.
OLIVIA

"Roll the 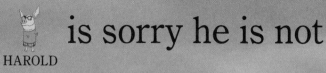 !"
VIDEO CAMERA

"This is Reporter  OLIVIA
live at the scene on ❄ day. SNOW
The Abominable ⛄ was SNOWMAN
captured in my backyard!
What a great ❄ day!" SNOW